GROWING UP

Written by: Louis McBride

With: Heddrick McBride

Illustrated by: Alex Baranov

Edited by: Jill McKellan

ISBN-10:1492245062

ISBN-13:978-1492245063

Every minute counts on the clock
when you are telling time.
One full minute is shown
by every single line.

The big numbers show you
a couple of things.
It will depend on which hand
that the arrow brings.

The big hand shows
that five minutes have passed.
The small hand shows
that for an hour it lasts.

There is a single line that never stops
and makes a tick-tock sound.
That line counts out sixty seconds
every time it makes it around.

You must value your time.
That is a very important fact.
It's the one thing, that once you lost it,
you can never get it back.

It's not good to be late for school;
your teachers call it tardy.
And you definitely don't want to be late
for a pizza party.

By the time you'd get there late
they wouldn't have any more food.
So besides being hungry,
you look very rude.

Being slow on the track
will make you lose the race.
One second can make the difference
between first and second place.

Always be on time for things,
but being early is also good.
This shows that for you the value
of time is understood.

If you were to count all the minutes in a day
it would be a large amount.
Treat each one with care
because every minute counts.

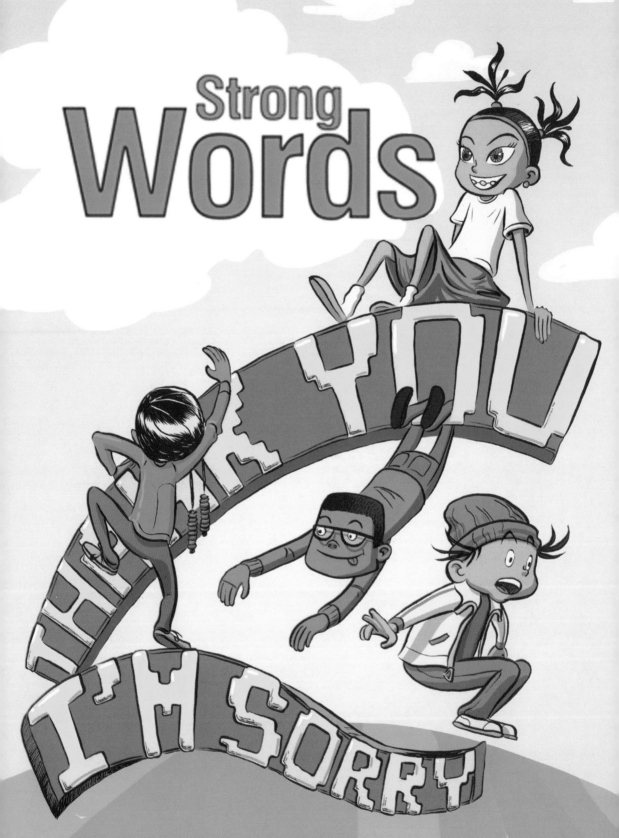

11

Strong words can help you reach your goals
if you don't forget them.
They can also make you feel really bad
if you let them.

There is great power in your words so be careful
how you choose them.
Please, thank you, I'm sorry.
Make sure that you always use them.

Words can explain to others
exactly how you feel.
It's important to use the right ones
to keep your message real.

Make sure that you are always honest
and always show respect.
The day that you hurt someone's feelings
is the one you'll regret.

Kind words to a friend or neighbor
can really make their day.
Good morning or you look nice today,
are some things you can say.

Promote fitness, health, sports,
and things that make people better.
It can be done by in person, on the internet,
or even in a letter.

Tell someone that you love them
and that you truly believe,
All of their goals, hopes, and dreams
they can definitely achieve.

You can inspire others by setting a positive example.
You must use strong words, but you also have to be careful.

Be careful not to use words that are insensitive or mean.
Evil words can destroy a person's hopes and dreams.

You should kindly tell others when they are right and when they are wrong.
You want them to overcome their problems and be strong.

When they are doing badly be sincere and honest.
They can do better; make sure that they promise.

Using strong words can make great changes that last forever.
Because when we use them wisely, they make all of our lives better.

VISITING ROOM

Last week, Dad and I
went to visit my Uncle Shane.
When he went to jail
it caused my family lots of pain.

Uncle Shane robbed a bank;
that's a very bad crime.
It has been two years,
but he still has to serve more time.

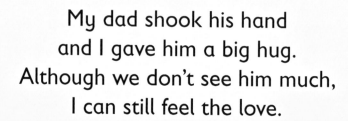

My dad shook his hand
and I gave him a big hug.
Although we don't see him much,
I can still feel the love.

He said he reads lots of books
and likes to exercise.
Now he wears glasses
because he has bad eyes.

He told me to stay out of trouble;
jail is no place to be.
I could be successful,
if I think positively.

Uncle Shane made me promise
to learn from his mistakes.
Losing a family member to prison
comes with plenty of heartaches.

Then he said that he was hungry so
I got him a snack from the lounge.
I bought him a sandwich
and some soda to wash it down.

There were other kids visiting their family that day. They were very nice, but no one was in the mood to play.

8:55 - 9:15

It was time for us to take some pictures of our trip.
Visiting time was over so we had to make it quick.

For my uncle to come home safely, every night I pray.
Until then we can only see him on Visiting Day.

Last week was the first time
my dad ever cried.
It was the day
that my great grandmother died.

She had breast cancer
and for two years, she quietly suffered.
Instead of breaking down,
it seemed like she got tougher.

She taught us lifetime lessons
about having pride and dignity.
These are messages for life
that I will always take with me.

All of the people at the funeral were
from many different generations.
Even though it was a sad day,
she deserved congratulations.

Great Grandma was a beautiful lady
that will live forever.
She had a beautiful heart
and made the best peach cobbler ever.

No one else will impress me like her,
no matter how hard they may try.

She taught herself to read and write
by using the Bible, that's why!

This lady was sweet as sugar,
but could also be very tough.
She kept the family together
when times got rough.

When I graduated from 5th grade
she made me a sweater.
She probably would have made me pants i
f I would have let her.

I told granny it was too hot for me
to wear matching flannels.
She smacked me in the back of the head
when she wanted me to change channels.

We shared memories that were so funny,
always making her laugh.
Sometimes she tried to spank us with the belt,
but we ran way too fast.

She was there when we needed help
or when we were feeling sick.
I always felt better after she made soup
or rubbed me down with Vicks.

She touched so many lives
that her spirit cannot die.
Great Grandma will always be with us
so we never have to say good bye.

VISIT
WWW.MCBRIDESTORIES.COM
FOR MORE TITLES

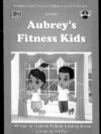